Keep me clean!

Please don't handle me with soiled hands.

Buddha  in the Garden

Buddha  in the Garden

David Bouchard

Paintings by
Zhong-Yang Huang

RAINCOAST BOOKS

Vancouver

The temple monks are wise and worthy. It is an honour to be a temple monk. They are considered holy and chosen. And all of them *are* chosen — all but the garden boy.

The monks often leave the temple. They are searching the world for enlightenment.

All of them travel around the world but two: the garden boy and the old blind monk who, day after day, sits meditating at the temple gate.

Years before, the garden boy had appeared at the temple gate, a small, abandoned bundle. The monks found him lying next to a bare root peony.

The monks who found the boy cared for him reluctantly. Raising an infant was not their purpose. Still, the child survived. And over time he came to live by the rules and customs of his solitary keepers.

But the boy was not allowed to think of enlightenment. The monks regarded the flower they had found lying next to him as a sign, and they made the boy their temple gardener.

Care of the garden is an important responsibility. In the quiet, dark morning, the garden boy shuffles through the temple gates weighted down with two large buckets of water. His eyes are on the ground. Then he hears the whisper of a man's voice.

Startled and frightened, he searches in one direction and then the other. There is no one to be seen but the blind old monk who never speaks a word to anyone.

The boy turns to leave when he hears the voice again.

"Buddha is in the garden!" says the voice.

Quickly, the garden boy spins around. Yes, it is the old monk who has spoken! The boy answers, "But Master, I have tended the garden every day for nine years and I have never seen nor heard Buddha. Perhaps only one who is worthy can see him? Perhaps the other monks, when they come for vegetables?"

The old monk says nothing. He merely sits.

The garden boy waits for a reply but none comes. After a short time, he hurries into the garden.

There, the boy searches every corner. It takes him only a moment to realize that Buddha is not in the garden.

He goes to his favourite resting spot, under a flowering tree next to his peony. There he sits, legs crossed. He turns the palms of his hands toward heaven, closes his eyes and begins dreaming.

In his dream, he sees a young woman propped up against a crumbling stone wall. Her face is gaunt and her eyes hollow. She hovers over a covered object, protecting it. Her pale, frail arms are wrapped tightly around her small package.

The boy opens his eyes to the sight of
a small, starving kitten. He is surprised;
animals are rarely seen in the temple.
The kitten is so thin that its ribs show
through its ragged coat.

The boy picks up the kitten and feeds it,
caring for it as the monks had cared for him.

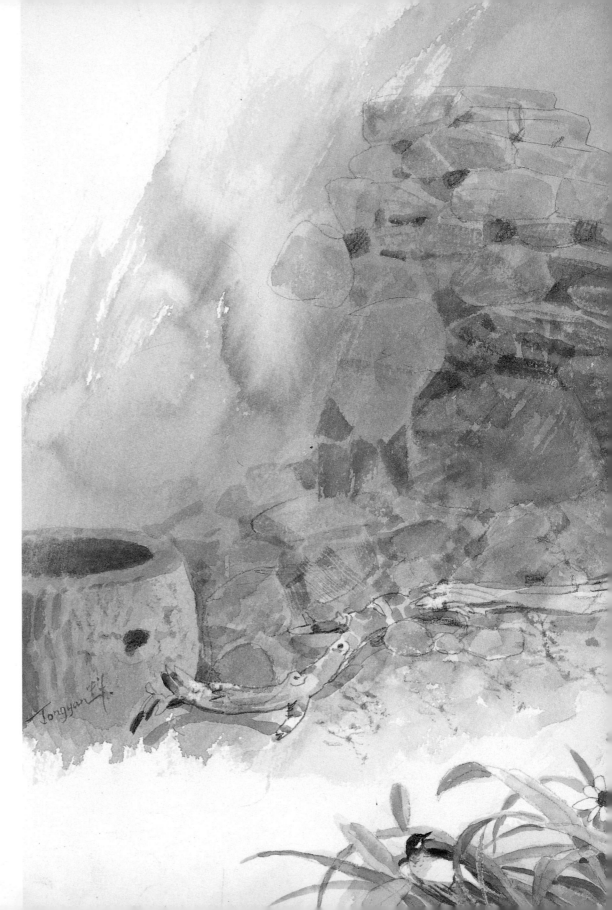

Weeks later, while passing through the gate again, the garden boy hears the old monk speak a second time: "Buddha is in the garden!" says the monk.

The boy quickly sits facing him.

"The last time you said that, Master, I went and I looked for him. I found nothing but a small, starving kitten. Master, where should I look? In what form will I find Buddha?"

After a few silent minutes, sensing that an answer will not come, the boy goes to his favourite resting spot. With the kitten curled up on his robe, he thinks about the old man's words.

Again, he dreams of the young woman. She is still near a crumbling wall, but this time she is crouched over, coughing feverishly, while her small bundle lies nestled on the ground at her feet.

A heavy, lonely feeling overcomes the boy.
He hears a light rustle and opens his eyes.

Next to his flower, he finds a small bird
trying to fly, but failing. Its wing is broken.
The boy picks up the bird, carries it to his
room and nurses it back to health.

Over the next few weeks, the garden boy spends part of each day sitting near the old monk. Hour after hour, he asks questions about life. He describes the beauty of his garden and of his peony. He describes every detail of his dreams: the beautiful woman— her hunger, her illness, and the bundle that consumes her so.

It is during one of these many visits that the old monk speaks again.

As the boy relates a long story about a bee that appears out of nowhere to hover in the garden, the old man interrupts.

"You have seen hunger and illness, boy. These are the first two signs. You will soon discover the third. Then you will find the enlightenment we are all seeking."

$\mathcal{S}$ensing this is a sign he might again
see the mysterious woman, the boy runs into
the garden. But as he approaches his special
place, he stops, frozen. He stares at his beautiful peony.

It is wilted, hanging lifeless from its stem. The
boy is not surprised by this death—each year
the flower dies and is reborn—but by the
strange timing of this event.

Quietly, the boy sits, closes his eyes and waits.

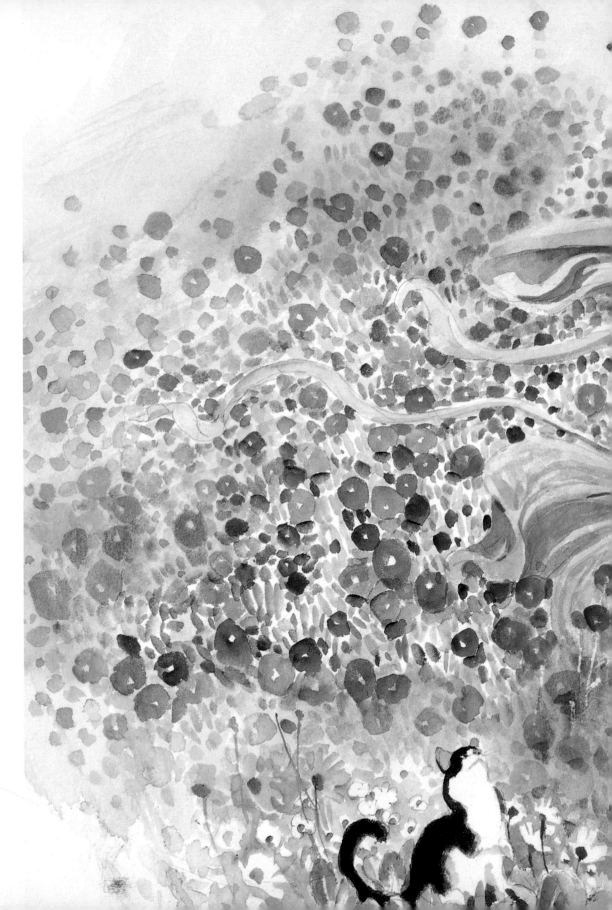

It is not long before the dream woman reappears. In her smile, the garden boy recognizes his own. For the first time, the woman turns and looks at him. Her voice is his voice: soft, kind, caring.

"I have longed to see you, my son. I have been here with you all these years, but now I must leave. You know hunger and you've seen illness. You also know that your flower has died and that it will live again. You now understand how we came to be apart. This is the third sign, child. It is the key to enlightenment."

Smiling tenderly, the dream woman walks toward her son and takes him in her arms.

As he sinks into his mother's embrace, the garden boy closes his eyes tight. He vows that nothing on earth or in heaven will ever take him from this place and this peace.

A few days later, seven monks return from their search for enlightenment in far-off lands. As they approach the gate, they hear the old monk speak.

"Buddha is in the garden," he says.

The seven monks hurry into the garden. Under the flowering tree, next to a dead peony, they discover the statue of a beautiful, young, smiling Buddha. His legs are crossed, his palms are turned toward heaven, and his eyes are shut tight.

There, silent before them, the seven monks see what they have been seeking all their lives: peace and fulfillment.

And on the smiling Buddha's lap, curled up as one, are a small frail kitten and a tiny bird.

The Story of the Buddha in the Garden

Buddhists will tell you that the Buddha in our story has been well depicted. They will say that a simple garden, high in the mountains, is a perfect place for Buddha. This is an ideal setting to allow you to understand something of enlightenment.

Our story is based on the four Buddhist signs of enlightenment: hunger, sickness, death and seeking enlightenment. Our story is ageless. It could have taken place 2,500 years ago, in the lifetime of the first recognized Buddha, Siddharta Gautama, or it could be happening in the Himalayan Mountains of today. Life there today is much as it was then. I have been there.

Much of our story has come from David's heart and mind, but not all of it. The old monk—he is real. A few of the others are also real. I saw them. I know them.

Several years ago, I went to a monastery. I was not seeking enlightenment. I was an artist in search of inspiration. The monks allowed me to live with them, under the condition that I live as they lived, that I follow their rules. Their rules were simple: I would not eat meat. I would live off the vegetables and plants grown in their garden. I would not use cooking oils, salt or any kind of additives that might

lessen the purity of my food. And I would only drink and wash with water that had fallen from heaven: rainwater.

At first, I managed fine. But after several weeks, I grew weak and sickly. It was a dry summer and we all washed from the same barrel of water. Over time, it had grown dirty. It stank. And it was difficult for me to eat as the monks did—day after day of tasteless vegetables. When I could not bear it any longer, I decided to walk several miles down the hill to the village. There, I bathed and I ate my fill.

That night, as I lay in my bed at the monastery, a monk knocked at my door. He told me that I would be asked to leave if I broke the rules again. The monks all knew what I had done because I stank of meat. I did not break the rules again nor did I stay much longer. However, I did stay long enough to paint much of what you see today.

The four signs of Buddhist enlightenment, they are real. And the old, blind monk—he is real. I sat across from him at the temple gate. I spent an entire day painting him. I did not ask his permission, nor did we speak—not a single word in the entire day. The only time I heard his voice was when I stood to leave. He said, "Thank you for spending this day with me, friend."

Zhong-Yang Huang